W9-CBI-892

# NASREDDIN HODJA

## ALPAY KABACALI

Illustrations by:

## FATİH M. DURMUŞ

**NET**®
TURİSTİK YAYINLAR
SANAYİ VE TİCARET A.Ş.

Published and distributed by:

**NET TURİSTİK YAYINLAR A.Ş.**

**Şifa Hamamı Sok. No. 18/2, 34400 Sultanahmet-İstanbul/Turkey**
**Tel: (90-212) 516 84 67 - 516 32 28 Fax: (90-212) 516 84 68**

**236. Sokak No.96/B Funda Apt., 35360 Hatay/İzmir/Turkey**
**Tel: (90-232) 228 78 51-250 69 22 Fax: (90-232) 250 22 73**

**Kışla Mah., 54. Sok., İlteray Apt., No.11/A-B, 07040 Antalya/Turkey**
**Tel: (90-242) 248 93 67 Fax: (90-242) 248 93 68**

**Eski Kayseri Cad., Dirikoçlar Apt. No.45, 50200 Nevşehir/Turkey**
**Tel: (90-384) 211 30 89 - 211 46 20 Fax: (90-384) 211 40 36**

Text: **Alpay Kabacalı**
Translation: **Nüket Eraslan**
Layout: **Not Ajans (Fatih M. Durmuş)**
Typesetting: **AS&64 Ltd. Şti.**
Colour separation: **Çali Grafik**
Printed in Turkey by: **Asır Matbaacılık Ltd. Şti.**

**ISBN 975-479-123-6**

Copyright © 1992 NET TURİSTİK YAYINLAR A.Ş.

All rights reserved.

4th Edition 1996

# CONTENTS

# NASREDDIN HODJA STORIES

**W**it, common sense, ingenuousness, ridicule… and the kind of humor that reflects human psychology, exposes the shortcomings of a society, criticizes even state and religious affairs yet always settles matters amicably are the elements which together create a special kind of logic, the Nasreddin Hodja logic. These features of the stories make the 13th century character Nasreddin Hodja immortal. Therefore, it is not an exaggeration to consider him one of the main building blocks of folk thought, and his humor, one of the best in the world.

Yet, it should be pointed out that these stories are related neither to Nasreddin Hodja himself nor to his historical personality. In other words, over the centuries many new stories where he was used as the main character have emerged, enriching the collection we have today. According to certain stories, Hodja was a contemporary of Tamerlane, who invaded Anatolia at the beginning of the 15th century, and according to the others, he lived either before or after the age of Tamerlane. Today, we still do not have historical documents that relate Hodja's life and his personality in depth.

The date 386 found inscribed on a gravestone attracted a lot of attention. Considering his humor, the date was read backwards. The year 683 of the Islamic calendar corresponds to theyears 1284-1285. Other documents were used to support the theory that he died sometime in the years 1284-1285. One of the most reliable document is the date 1383 (796 in the Islamic calendar) found inscribed on the wall of his tomb in Akşehir. It indicates that Hodja died before 1393 and his tomb had been visited for years.

The town of Sivrihisar of the city of Eskişehir is accepted as the birthplace of Hodja. A gravestone dated 1327 found in Sivrihisar, belongs to his daughter Fatima and indicates that she lived 43 more years after his death.

The oldest Nasreddin Hodja story is found in the book called *"Saltukname"* written in 1480, which also contains other folk stories and legends. It is stated in "Saltukname" that Hodja was born in Sivrihisar and that the natives of Sivrihisar were famous for their strange behavior and ingenousness. The strange behavior of the natives of Sivrihisar is also mentioned in a handwritten story book in Biblioteque Nationale in Paris. These documents are considered proof of his birth in Sivrihisar.

Based on the above mentioned documents and certain stories, following is the life story of Nasreddin Hodja:

He was born in the village of Hortu of Sivrihisar and died in 1284 in Akşehir, a province of Konya, where his tomb is. His father was the imam (religious leader) of the village. Hodja, himself, too, served as the imam of the village for a period

# The Tomb of Nasreddin Hodja (Akşehir).

of time and later went to Akşehir to become the dervish of the two very famous Islamic mystics of the time. In his life time he also served as a judge and university professor.

As mentioned before, according to certain sources, he was a contemporary of Tamerlane, who invaded Anatolia in 1301, but according to the others a person named Nasreddin Hodja never lived; he was just an imaginary character in the folk stories.

It is obvious that Hodja was a witty man with a sense of humor and he was a good conversationalist. Yet, based on most of the stories it is wrong to assume that everything he said was humorous. Over the years, the number of Nasreddin Hodja stories increased significantly since he was used as the main character in the new stories about other people. Among these, there are some that are easily recognized as not authentic Nasreddin Hodja stories. We can, therefore, say that Hodja and his stories were created by the natives of Anatolia in the 13th century, and the creation has lasted for centuries. Today, these stories belong to all Turkish people.

The themes of the stories cover not just the age when Nasreddin Hodja lived but also the adventures of Turkish people over the centuries. As one of our writers said "Nasreddin Hodja is the only person who lived both before his birth and after his death. There are many historical and social personalities who kept on living after their death but the only person on earth who lived before his birth is Nasreddin Hodja" Therefore, social life, the short-comings of social life, differences between the ruling class and the common people, famines, the thousand faces of daily life, man to man, man to object, man to animal relations are the different themes of the stories and in all of these stories Nasreddin Hodja is a symbol.

Nasreddin Hodja stories were spread by word of mouth over a vast area mainly in the lands under the domain of the Ottoman Empire and the lands where Turkish was spoken. In certain countries, the Hodja character was almost his "twin brother" or a "competitor", and it other countries only the name Nasreddin Hodja was modified in the stories. Today, Nasreddin Hodja stories are told in a vast geographic area extending from East Turkmenistan to Hungary and from Southern Siberia to North Africa. The stories have been translated into many languages.

The new Nasreddin Hodja stories that emerge and the old ones that are adapted prove that these stories are immortal. On the other hand, it is stated that since these stories, products of the imagination of common people, are adaptable it is natural that they are updated in each generation and

A Nasreddin Hodja miniature taken from a XVII the century hand written book
(Topkapı Palace Museum Library Cat. No. 2142).

that is why Nasreddin Hodja is still the most popular story character in Turkey. In other words, as light attracts moths, Nasreddin Hodja character attracts new stories.

Nasreddin Hodja stories are told in such succinct phrases that the last phrase of the stories which is uttered by Hodja have become popular epigrams or sayings like "laying flour on rope," "making it look like a bird," "the quilt is gone, the fight is over," "cutting the branch one is sitting on," etc.

Every year, between July 5-10, International Nasreddin Hodja Festival is organized in Akşehir where his tomb is. To keep Hodja character alive, Turkish writers and artists have used it in drama, in music, in movies (especially cartoons), in comic strips, in paintings.

After reading the stories in this book, we think that you, too, will believe that Hodja will be living for generations to come.. Just as Hodja did, may be you, too, will answer when asked "What do they do with the old full moons?", "They cut them up into small pieces and make stars!.."

Even in this Space Age!..

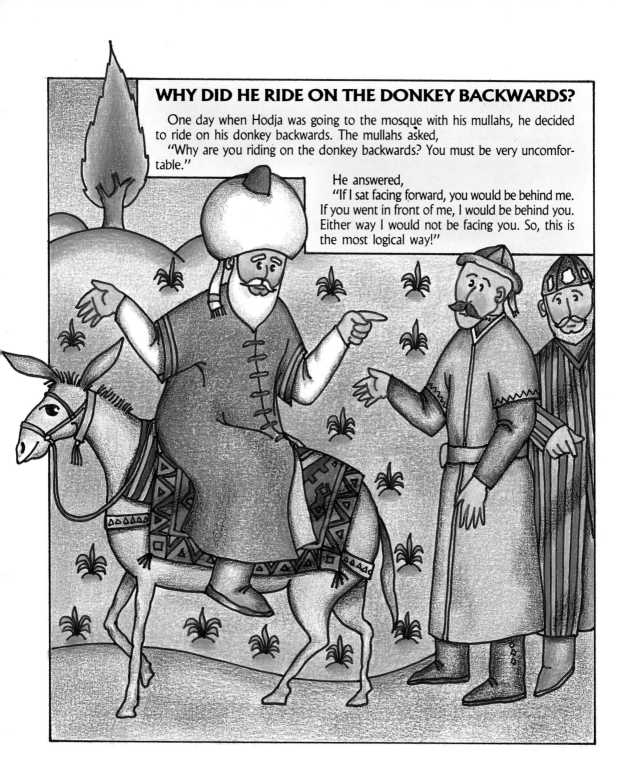

# WHY DID HE RIDE ON THE DONKEY BACKWARDS?

One day when Hodja was going to the mosque with his mullahs, he decided to ride on his donkey backwards. The mullahs asked,

"Why are you riding on the donkey backwards? You must be very uncomfortable."

He answered,

"If I sat facing forward, you would be behind me. If you went in front of me, I would be behind you. Either way I would not be facing you. So, this is the most logical way!"

## EVERYONE WHO SEES THE LIGHT...

Hodja's wife was pregnant. One night, her labor pains started and Hodja called the neighbours and the midwife. Soon they called out from his wife's room and said,

"Hodja! You have a son!"

He was very happy. A few minutes later the midwife called out again,

"Hodja! You also have a girl."

After a little while, she called out again,

"Hodja! You have another girl!"

Hodja, who had been waiting in front of his wife's room, rushed into the room and blew off the candle.

"What are you doing?" asked the surprised women.

"Well! Everyone who sees the light wants to come out. What else can I do?" he answered.

## FORTY YEAR OLD VINEGAR

His neighbour asked Hodja,

"Do you have some forty-year old vinegar?"

"I have," answered Hodja.

"Would you give me some? I need it to prepare a medication," said the man.

"No, I won't," replied Hodja. "If I had given some to everybody who asked for it, would I have it for forty years."

## MORTAL'S WAY

One day four boys approached Hodja and gave him a bagful of walnuts.

"Hodja, we can't divide these walnuts among us evenly. So would you help us, please?"

Hodja asked,

"Do you want God's way of distribution or mortal's way?"

"God's way," the children answered.

Hodja opened the bag and gave two handfuls of walnuts to one child, one handful to the other, only two walnuts to the third child and none to the fourth.

"What kind of distribution is this?" the children asked baffled.

"Well, this is God's way," he answered. "He gives some people a lot, some people a little and nothing to others. If you had asked for mortal's way I would have given the same amount to everybody."

# HOW A DONKEY READS!

During a conversation with Tamerlane, Hodja started bragging about his donkey.

"It is so smart that I can teach it even how to read," he said.

"Then go ahead and teach it how read. I give you 3 months," Tamerlane ordered.

Hodja went home and began to train his donkey. He put its feed between the pages of a big book and taught it to turn the pages by its tongue to find its feed. Three days before the three month period was over, he stopped feeding it.

When he took his donkey to Tamerlane, he asked for a big book and put it in front of the donkey. The hungry animal turned the pages of the book one by one with its togue and when it couldn't find any feed between the pages it started braying.

Tamerlane watched the donkey closely and then said,

"This sure is a strange way of reading!"

Hodja remarked,

"But this is how a donkey reads."

# WE ARE EVEN

One day, Hodja went to a Turkish bath but nobody paid him much attention. They gave him an old bath robe and a towel. Hodja said nothing and on his way out he left a big tip. A week later, when he went back to the same bath, he was very well received. Everybody tried to help him and offered him extra services. On his way out, he left a very small tip.

"But, Hodja," they said, "Is it fair to leave such a small tip for all the attention and extra services you received?"

Hodja answered,

"Today's tip is for last week's services and last week's tip was for today's services. Now we are even."

## INEXPERIENCED NIGHTINGALE

One day when he was young, Hodja climbed a fig tree and started eating the figs. Soon he was caught by the owner of the land. The man asked,

"Hey! Who are you? What are you doing up there in my tree?"

"I am a nightingale," Hodja answered.

"If you are a nightingale, let's hear you sing," the man replied.

Hodja made strange sounds trying to imitate a nightingale.

"What kind of a nightingale are you? Nightingales don't sing like this!" said the man.

"Well," said Hodja, "this is how inexperienced nightingales sing."

## NO NEED FOR SO MUCH FUSS

Every time Hodja's wife decided to do the laundry, it rained.

"I've found the solution," Hodja said one day. "We are not going to let God know which day we do the laundry."

"How?" asked his wife.

"Well, when the weather is good, you give me a signal. I'll go to the store, buy soap and other necessary items. We will take care of this without talking to each other."

A few days later, his wife signalled to Hodja that she was going to do the laundry. He went to the store and bought the necessary items. When he came out of the store it was raining lightly. He signed and looked up to the sky. Suddenly, there was lightning and thunder. Hodja hid what he had bought under his robe and said,

"There is no need for so much fuss. We were not going to wash the laundry anyway."

## SHOULD HAVE HIS OWN DONKEY

Hodja tied his donkey to a pole by the courthouse and went to the marketplace. In the mean time, the judge decided that the false witness being persecuted be punished by having him ride on a donkey backwards in the streets of the town. So, they used Hodja's donkey for the punishment. When Hodja came back and didn't find his donkey, he got furious.

After sometime the same man was punished the same way for the same offense. When they could't find a donkey to carry on the punishment, they wanted to borrow Hodja's donkey and sent him a messenger. Hodja was fed up.

"I won't give you my donkey! You go and tell that man either to give up this business or get himself a donkey in case he needs it again," he said.

## WHAT IF IT HAPPENS

When they saw Hodja sitting by the lake and stirring some yogurt into the water they asked him what he was doing.

"I am adding starter into the lake to make yogurt," he answered.

"But is it possible to turn the lake into yogurt?"

"I know it is impossible but what if I succeed," Hodja replied.

19

## LET THEM SEE ME TRADING

Hodja used to buy nine eggs for one akçe and then sell ten for one.
"Hodja, what kind of trading is this?" they asked.

"Well, look at the other sellers and look at me. I am surrounded by customers. Is there anything more satisfying than this? I am not a cheat; I just want friends see me buying and selling things, that's all."

## THANK GOD

One of his friends saw Hodja carrying a basket of beets.
"Where are you going with this?" he asked.

"I am going to give it to Tamerlane as a present," Hodja answered.

"You better take him figs. Tamerlane doesn't like beets," his friend warned him.

Hodja took his friends advice and gave a basket of figs to Tamerlane. But Tamerlane hated figs, too. As soon as he saw them, he ordered Hodja to be punished.

"Hit him on the head with each fig," he ordered.

While the soldiers were throwing the figs at him, each time a fig hit his head, Hodja said,

"Thank God!"

Tamerlane asked,

"Why do you thank God every time a fig hits your head?"

"Thank God," Hodja repeated. "If I hadn't listen to my friend and brought you the beets anyway, what would have happened to me?"

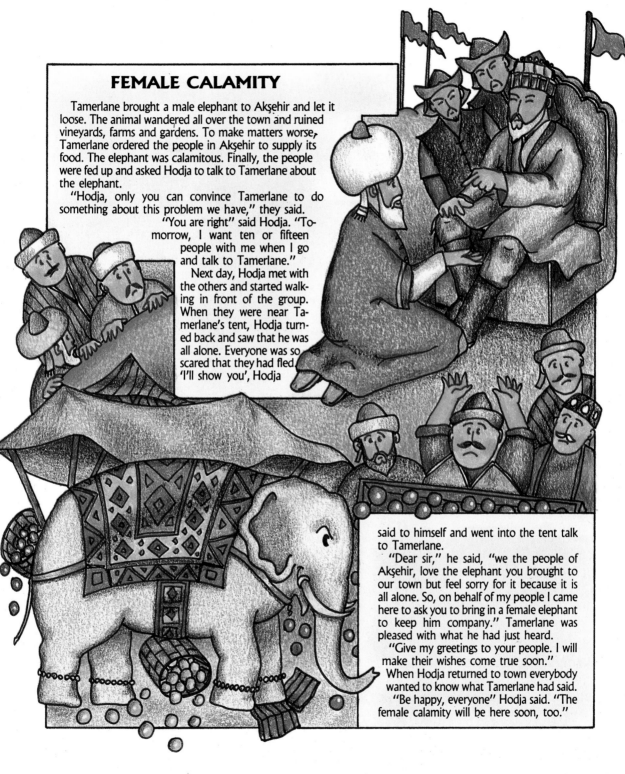

# FEMALE CALAMITY

Tamerlane brought a male elephant to Akşehir and let it loose. The animal wandered all over the town and ruined vineyards, farms and gardens. To make matters worse, Tamerlane ordered the people in Akşehir to supply its food. The elephant was calamitous. Finally, the people were fed up and asked Hodja to talk to Tamerlane about the elephant.

"Hodja, only you can convince Tamerlane to do something about this problem we have," they said.

"You are right" said Hodja. "Tomorrow, I want ten or fifteen people with me when I go and talk to Tamerlane."

Next day, Hodja met with the others and started walking in front of the group. When they were near Tamerlane's tent, Hodja turned back and saw that he was all alone. Everyone was so scared that they had fled. 'I'll show you', Hodja said to himself and went into the tent talk to Tamerlane.

"Dear sir," he said, "we the people of Akşehir, love the elephant you brought to our town but feel sorry for it because it is all alone. So, on behalf of my people I came here to ask you to bring in a female elephant to keep him company." Tamerlane was pleased with what he had just heard.

"Give my greetings to your people. I will make their wishes come true soon."

When Hodja returned to town everybody wanted to know what Tamerlane had said.

"Be happy, everyone" Hodja said. "The female calamity will be here soon, too."

## DIDN'T KNOW HOW TO LAND PROPERLY

One day Hodja was walking along his donkey by a cliff. His donkey tripped, lost it's balance and fell off the cliff. The poor animal hit the bottom and was torn to pieces. Hodja looked down at the corps of his donkey for awhile and then said,

"Apparently, it had learned how to fly, but not to land properly."

## I KNOW WHAT I'LL DO

Hodja lost his saddlebag in the town he stopped to spend the night.

"You either find my saddlebag or I know what I'll do," he said to the peasants in town.

The peasants were alarmed, and they looked for it everywhere. They finally found Hodja's saddlebag and returned it to him. Just before Hodja left the town, the peasants asked,

"What would you have done if we hadn't found it?"

Hodja shrugged his shoulders and said,

"I have an old kilim at home. I was going to cut it up and make a saddlebag with it."

## TASTE THE SAME

When the children of the neighbourhood saw Hodja coming from the vineyard with 2 basketfuls of grapes on his donkey, they gathered around him and asked him to give them some. Hodja picked up a bunch of grapes, cut it up into pieces and gave each child a piece.

"You have so much, but you gave us so little," the children complained.

"It doesn't make any difference whether you have a basketful or a small piece. They all taste the same," Hodja remarked.

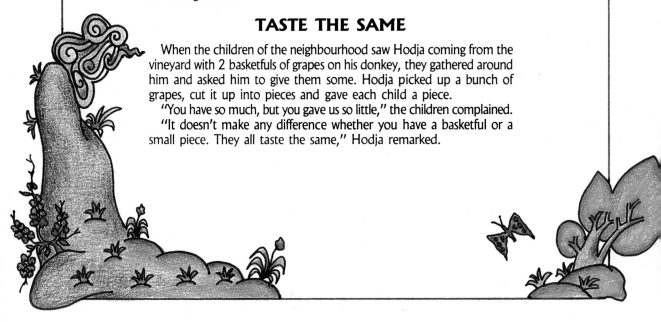

## DUCK SOUP

Hodja saw a group of ducks in the lake. He tried to catch one but couldn't succeed. So, he sat by the lake and took out a loaf of bread from his saddlebag. He broke it into pieces, started dunking them into the water and eating them. A passerby saw Hodja and asked him what he was eating. Hodja dunked another piece in and said, "Duck soup."

## EARTH'S BALANCE

They asked Hodja,

"Sir, in the morning some people go this way and some go the opposite way. Why?"

Hodja answered,

"If they all went in the same direction, the Earth would loose its balance and topple."

## IF I WERE ON IT...

Hodja had lost his donkey. While he was looking for, it he kept repeating,

"Thank God!"

"Hodja, why are you thanking God all the time?" people asked.

"I am grateful that I was not on the donkey. Otherwise I would be lost, too," he aswered.

## IF IT IS UP TO THE TURBAN AND THE ROBE

An Iranian gave Hodja the letter he had received from a friend back home and asked Hodja to read it to him. Hodja looked at the letter. It was in Persian and the handwriting was terrible. So, he told the man,

"Have somebody else read it."

The man insisted.

"Listen! I don't know Persian. Even if it were in Turkish, the writing is so bad that I still would't be able to read it," Hodja explained.

The Iranian got mad,

"You are wearing a huge robe and a turban but can't read even a simple letter. You should be ashamed of yourself!"

Hodja took off his turban and robe, and gave them to the Iranian.

"If one can do anything by wearing a robe and a turban, then here, you wear them and read the letter yourself," he added.

## THEN, WHERE IS THE CAT

A few times Hodja brought home some meat but never got a chance to eat it. His wife either ate it herself or gave it to her friends, and each time Hodja asked for some meat she said,

"The cat stole it. I ran after it but I couldn't catch it."

One day when his wife again told him that the cat had eaten the 2 kilos of meat he had brought, Hodja grabbed the cat and weighed it. It weighed 2 kilos. Hodja then turned to his wife and said,

"If this is the cat then where is the meat? But if this the meat, then, where is the cat?"

## REMEMBERED IT'S CHILDHOOD

Some of the children in the neighbourhood snatched Hodja's turban, and when he tried to get it back, they started passing it from one to another. Realizing that he wasn't going to succeed in getting it back, he went home.. When his wife asked,

"Hodja, where is your turban?"

"It remembered its childhood so, it is playing with the children," he answered.

## HAVE IT PULLED OUT

When a man asked Hodja,

"I have terrible headaches.. What do you think I should do?"

Hodja replied,

"A few days ago, I had a terrible toothache. Nothing helped so I had it pulled out and now I am fine."

## WITH THIS HUGE BOWL

From time to time Hodja used to invite his mullahs to his house for dinner. One day, he invited them again and they all came. Hodja's wife called him to the kitchen and said,

"There is no rice, no butter. As a matter of fact, there is not a bite to eat. We don't even have wood to burn."

Hodja grabbed a big bowl, walked into the living room, showed it to the mullahs and said,

"Sorry! But if we had rice, butter and wood to burn, we would cook soup and serve it to you in this huge bowl."

## CHARGE FOR TEN DAYS

Hodja gathered up the old and seldom-used items in his house to sell them in the marketplace. He asked a man to carry the load but on the way to the marketplace he lost sight of the man. He looked for him everywhere but couldn't find him.

A few days later when Hodja saw the man coming down the road he started running away. A friend saw him and asked,

"Hodja, you were looking for this man for sometime. Now that you have seen him, why are you running away?"

"Why shouldn't I? What if he charges me for the last ten days!" Hodja replied.

## FORCE YOU TO EAT

Hodja went to Konya on business but he had no money. As he pass-ed by a helva (a sweet prepared by sesame oil) sellers store, he got a yen for some helva. So, he went in the store, grabbed a big piece and began to eat. The owner came up to him and started yelling,

"How dare you help yourself to the helva without asking or paying for it?"

When Hodja ignored him and kept on eating, the man really got mad and started hitting and kicking him. Hodja kept on eating, and said to the customers who were watching what was happening,

"The natives of Konya are such good people. They hit you and they kick you to force you to eat some of their delicious helva."

## NOT TO LEAVE HIS HEAD

One of the richest businessmen in town invited Hodja to his house. Hodja went to the man's house on the day they had decided. As he approached the house Hodja saw the man sitting by the window. He rang the door bell and said,

"I am here to pay a visit to the master."

The housekeeper told Hodja that the master of the house was not in. Hodja got irritated but remained calm.

"Then give him my regards and please tell him not to leave his head by the window the next time he leaves home," he said.

## TO CLIMB HILLS...

Hodja was getting old and having a hard time making ends meet. One day, they asked him,

"Hodja, why did God create men?"

Hodja answered without hesitation,

"So they climb hills and pay debts."

# A PAN OF BAKLAVA

When a foreign scholar came to Akşehir and asked to talk to the wisest man in town, they called Hodja. When they met, the man drew a circle on the ground with a long stick. Then, Hodja got the stick and drew a straight line dividing the circle into two equal parts.. The man then drew a line perpendicular to the one Hodja had drawn, thus dividing the circle into 4 equal parts. Hodja gestured like he was taking the three parts and leaving the fourth to the scholar. Then, the stranger brought the fingers of his right hand together and shook his hand pointing towards the ground. Hodja did just the opposite; he strecthed out his fingers.

When the meeting was over, the scholar explained:

"Your Hodja is very smart. When I told him that the Earth is round, he said that the equator divides it into two. When I divided the Earth into four sections, he said that three fourths of it is water and one fourth of it is land.. When I asked him what causes rain, he told me that water evaporates, vapor rises, forms clouds and then turns into rain."

Then, they asked Hodja what happened during the meeting and this is what he told:

"That glutton! He said, 'Let's have a pan of baklava' I told him, 'You can't eat it alone. I will eat half of it'. 'What would you do, if I divide it into four?' he asked and I told him, 'I would eat three fourths of it'. Then he said 'Let's sprinkle some nuts on it'. I said 'O.K. but you can't do it on hot ashes, you need flaming fire for it.' He couldn't go on any more, so he left."

# THE QUILT IS GONE AND THE FIGHT IS OVER

Hodja and his wife were awakened by noises coming from the street. When he looked out the window, he saw two people fighting. He took his quilt, wrapped it around himself and started walking towards the door. Although his wife told him not to get involved, he ignored her.

"Let's see what is going on," he said and went out.

As soon as he stepped out the door, before he had a chance to find out what was happening, one of the man pulled the quilt off his back and fled. The other one disappeared in the dark.

Hodja looked after them for a few minutes and then went inside, freezing. His wife asked, "What was he fight about?"

"I don't know what it was all about, but all I know is that the quilt is gone and the fight is over," Hodja replied.

# LOOK WHAT YOU GAVE

One hot summer day, Hodja had to go to a nearby town. After walking for hours under the hot sun, he got tired. He sat under a tree and said, 'Oh, Lord, I wish you would give your servant, Hodja, a donkey to ride on so he would't get so tired walking in the sun in his old age.' A few minutes later he saw a cavalry soldier, with a 6 month old colt walking along him, approaching him. He came up to Hodja and ordered,

"Hey, you! Don't just sit there and be lazy. My colt is tired of walking. So, get up and carry him on your back to the next town."

Hodja tried to explain to him that he was old and tired but the soldier wouldn't listen. He even gave Hodja a whip on the back. Hodja had no choise but carry the colt to the town. When they finally reached their destination, Hodja put the colt down and collapsed. After awhile he pulled himself together, sat up, raised his hands and said,

"My Lord, either I couldn't express myself right or you misunderstood me. I asked for something to ride on but you gave me something which rode on me!.."

# EAT, MY FUR COAT, EAT!

Hodja was invited to a dinner reception. He put on his old robe and went. When he noticed that nobody paid him any attetion, he rushed back home, put on his new robe and fur coat, and returned to the reception. This time, they greeted him at the door, escorted him to the table and offered him the most delicious dishes. Each time they placed a plateful of food in front of him, he dipped the collar of his fur coat into the food and said,

"Eat, my fur coat, eat!"

Everybody was surprised. So, they asked,

"What are you doing, Hodja?"

"Since all this attention and generosity is extended to my fur coat, it might as well eat the food, too," he answered.

## TRIED HARD BUT...

Hodja had an ox with horns shaped like a bow. He always wanted to sit between the horns and ride the ox but he was afraid. One day, he saw the ox sleeping. He quietly approached it and managed to sit between the horns. The animal was startled. It shook and threw Hodja to the ground. He fell on his head and passed out. When his wife saw him lying on the ground motionless, she thought he was dead and began to cry. Soon, Hodja opened his eyes and consoled his wife,

"Don't cry, my dear. I tried hard, got badly hurt but I finally did what I had always wanted to do."

## SUCH BIG MISTAKES

Carrying weapons was prohibited but Hodja had a big curved knife and one day, he was caught carrying it into the Medrese (theological school). When the the guard asked him what he was going to do with it Hodja replied,

"With this, I scrape off the mistakes I see in the books."

(In those days they used to use small knives to scrape off the mistakes).

The guard got irritated.

"You liar! You don't need such a big knife for that."

"Oh! You don't know, sir. Sometimes there are such big mistakes that even this knife is not big enough," Hodja replied.

## I WAS IN IT

One morning, his neighbour asked Hodja,

"Last night we heard noises coming from your house. It sounded like something falling down the stairs. What happened?"

Hodja replied,

"My wife threw my robe down the stairs."

"Come on, Hodja! A robe doesn't make that much noise."

"But I was wearing it," Hodja said.

## LET US DIE, TOO

One hot summer night they invited Hodja to dinner. The first course was ice cold compote. The mischevious host picked up a ladle and began to drink the compote. After he finished each ladleful, he exclaimed,

"Oh, I am dying!"

Hodja and the other guests were using small spoons and they could neither get the taste of the compote nor quench their thirst.

Finally, Hodja lost his patience and called out to his host,

"Sir, why don't you let us use the ladle so we get a chance to die, too, at least once."

## RUN TO THE LAKE

One winter day, Hodja gathered up wood and loaded it on his donkey. On the way home he wandered whether the load of wood he had gathered was dry enough to burn. He decided to burn a few pieces to check. Before he knew what was happening the whole load caught on fire. Startled by the fire, his donkey began to run away. He looked after his donkey and yelled,

"If I were you, I would run to the lake!"

## OUT OF EMBARRASSMENT

When Hodja heard the footsteps of a thief in his house, he hid in the closet where they kept the bed clothes. The thief looked all over the house but found nothing of value to steal. Hoping to find something there, he opened the door of the closet and came face to face with Hodja. The thief was surprised and asked,

"Oh! What are you doing here?"

"Sorry," said Hodja nonchalantly. "Since there is nothing worth stealing in this house, I was so embarrassed that I hid in the closet."

## THOSE WHO KNOW TEACH

Hodja went to the pulpit and before he started his sermon he asked the congregation,

"Do you know what I will be talking about today?"

"No," answered the congregation.

"If you don't know then what can I tell you?" he replied and walked away.

Next week, he went to the pulpit and asked the same question.

This time the congregation answered,

"Yes, we do."

"If you do, then there is nothing I can tell you," Hodja said and walked away again.

Members of the congregation decided that if Hodja asked the same question again half of them would say "yes" and the other half would say "no."

The following week, Hodja went to the pulpit and asked the same question again. As they had decided, half of them said, "Yes, we do" and the other half said "No, we don't."

"In that case, those who know tell the ones who don't know," said Hodja and walked away again.

35

## SETTLE FOR NINE

Hodja was dreaming somebody had given him nine gold pieces and he was asking for one more to have ten pieces. Then he woke up. He immediately looked in his hands and when he didn't see any coins, he closed his eyes tight, stretched out his hand and said,

"O.K., O.K. Bring back the money. I'll settle for nine."

## CASH MONEY

Hodja had borrowed money from a friend but couldn't pay it back on time. One day, when his friend came back again to ask for his money Hodja said,

"I'll pay you back soon."

"When?" asked the man.

"Now, listen well. You see, I have planted bushes in front of my house. Come spring, these bushes will grow taller."

"Yes!"

"The sheep that pass by my house will rub against the bushes and their wool will be caught on the branches."

"Oh?"

"Then, I will gather up the wool, roll it, take it to the market, sell it and then pay you the money I owe."

When his friend started laughing, Hodja said,

"You, devil you! You already feel the cash in your hands and you are happy, aren't you?"

## MAKE STARS

On a beautiful starry night, Hodja was watching the new moon in the sky.

"What do they do with the old full moons?" somebody asked.

"They cut them up into pieces, crumble them and make stars," Hodja answered.

## JUST AN ORDINARY...

One day Hodja went to the mill. While he was waiting for his turn, he kept on taking handfuls of wheat from the other sacks and putting them into his. When the miller noticed what Hodja was doing, he got very mad and started screaming,

"What do you think you are doing?"

Hodja replied nonchalantly, "I am an idiot. I do whatever comes to my mind."

"Really! Then why don't you take some from your own and put into other sacks," the man said angrily.

"But, Sir, I am just an ordinary idiot. If I did that I would be a super idiot," Hodja said calmly.

# IF THE ANGEL OF DEATH COMES

Hodja was seriously ill and was getting worse. He called his wife and said,

"Now, go and put make-up on, wear your new dress and lots of jewellery. Then, come and sit by me."

His wife was shocked.

"Hodja, you are so ill and I don't feel like getting dressed up and looking good. Do you think I have no scruples?" she asked.

"Oh, no! You misunderstood me," Hodja answered, "I will be dying soon. So, when the angel of death comes, it may like you better than me and take you instead, I thought."

# CENTER OF THE EARTH

Three scholarly priests, who were travelling the world, came to Akşehir to talk to Hodja whose world-wide reputation they had heard of. Hodja was introduced to the priests at a meeting attended by the most respectable men in town. After a pleasant dinner, they chatted for awhile and then one of the priests asked Hodja,

"Hodja, where is the center of the Earth?"

Pointing to his donkey standing in front of the door, Hodja said,

"It is under the front feet of my donkey."

"How do you know?" the priest asked.

"If you don't believe me, go and measure," Hodja replied.

Then the second priest asked,

"Hodja, how many starts are there in the sky?"

"There are as many stars as the bristles on my donkey's tail," he answered.

"How can you prove it?" the priest continued.

"Well, if you don't believe me, go and count them," Hodja replied.

The priests were so baffled by the quick answers of Hodja that the third one changed his mind about asking him a question.

# SMOKE SELLER

In the marketplace of Akşehir, a poor man was passing by a grilled meat vendor, and he got a yen for some grilled meat. Since he couldn't afford to buy the meat, he took out a few pieces of bread from his pocket, held them in the smoke coming off the grill and ate them. As he was leaving, the vendor grabbed him and said,

"You cannot leave without paying!"

The man refused to pay and when they couldn't settle the argument, they went to see the judge, Nasreddin Hodja.

Hodja listened to both sides. Then turned to the poor man and said,

"Give me all your money."

The poor man was surprised but gave Hodja his bag of money anyway. Hodja emptied the bag onto the table, counted the coins one by one and then turned to the vendor,

"Have you heard to sound of the coins?" he asked.

"Yes, I have," answered the man.

Hodja put the coins back into the bag, returned it to the poor man and said to the vendor,

"The price of smoke is sound of coins. You sold smoke and in return you heard the sound of the coins. Therefore, you have been paid."

## WHAT'S KEEPING YOU...

Hodja was very hungry by the time he arrived in Konya but he had no money to buy food. He stopped in front of the window of a bakery and saw many fresh loaves of bread. He entered the store and pointing to the loaves of bread, asked the owner,

"Are these all yours?"

"Yes, they are mine," answered the owner.

"Are you sure that they are all yours?" Hodja asked again.

The baker got irritated and said angrily,

"Yes, I am sure!"

"If all of these delicious smelling loaves of bread are yours then why don't you go ahead and eat them? What's keeping you?"

## IT IS DARK IN THERE

Hodja lost his ring in the basement of his house. He looked for it but when he could't find it, he went in front of the door of his house and started looking for it there. His neighbour asked,

"Hodja, what are you looking for?"

"I lost my ring."

"Where did you lose it?"

"I dropped it in the basement," Hodja answered.

The man was surprised.

"Then why aren't you looking for it there?"

"Well, it is so dark in there that I can't see a thing. That's why I am looking for it here."

# THE BROTH OF THE BROTH

A peasant from another town came to visit Hodja and brought a rabbit as a present. Hodja cooked the rabbit and served it to the peasant. He also asked the man to spend the night at his home.

Next week, the man returned. Hodja invited him to dinner and asked him to spend the night at his home again. When he served the soup he jokingly said,

"This soup is made with the broth of the rabbit you brought last week." The following week, two other peasants come to visit Hodja and told him,

"We are the friends of the man who brought you a rabbit two weeks ago."

Hodja invited them to dinner and asked them to spend the night, too.

A week later a few more peasants from the same town came over and told Hodja the same thing. Hodja asked them to stay for dinner and served them water. The men were very surprised.

"Sir, what is this?" they asked.
"This is the broth of the broth of the rabbit which your friend brought me" Hodja answered.

41

# WHO NEEDS THE SOAP MORE!

Hodja and his wife gathered up their dirty clothes and took them to the river to be washed. His wife had taken the only bar of soap in the house to do the laundry. While she was filling the bucket with water from the river, a crow flew away with the bar of soap which was resting on top of the clothes.

"Run Hodja! A crow stole our only bar of soap," she screamed.

Hodja looked after the crow and said,

"Let it have it. Can't you see that what it is wearing is dirtier than our laundry."

## WITH THE LUCK YOU BROUGHT!

One of the sadistic landlords of Akşehir went to a village nearby for a few days. Upon his return, Hodja and a few other people went to his house to welcome him back. When they asked him whether he had enjoyed his stay there, the man said,

"I had a lot of fun. On Monday, there was a big fire and two people burned to death. Next day, a rabid dog bit three people and I treated their wounds by a hot branding iron. On Wendsday, it rained so hard that there was flooding. A few houses collapsed and many animals were washed away by floods. On Thursday, an angry bull rampaged through the town killing two people. On Friday, a peasant went crazy and cut his wife and child to pieces. I had him tortured and killed in the town square. On Saturday, a house collapsed and the few people inside died. On Sunday, we went to watch the woman who had strangled her child to death hang herself from a tree. So, you see, I had fun everyday of the week."

Hodja couldn't contain himself anymore and said,

"Good thing you came back early. With the luck you had brought to that town, there wouldn't be an erect stone or a live person left in it.

## THE FEELING OF FINDING

One day, Hodja lost his donkey again. He rushed to the marketplace and announced,

"Whoever finds and brings my donkey to me will have it, including its saddle."

Everybody was surprised.

"If you are going to give your donkey to the person who finds it then why are you looking for it?" they asked.

"But, ah!!" said Hodja, "You don't know how good it feels to find something you've lost."

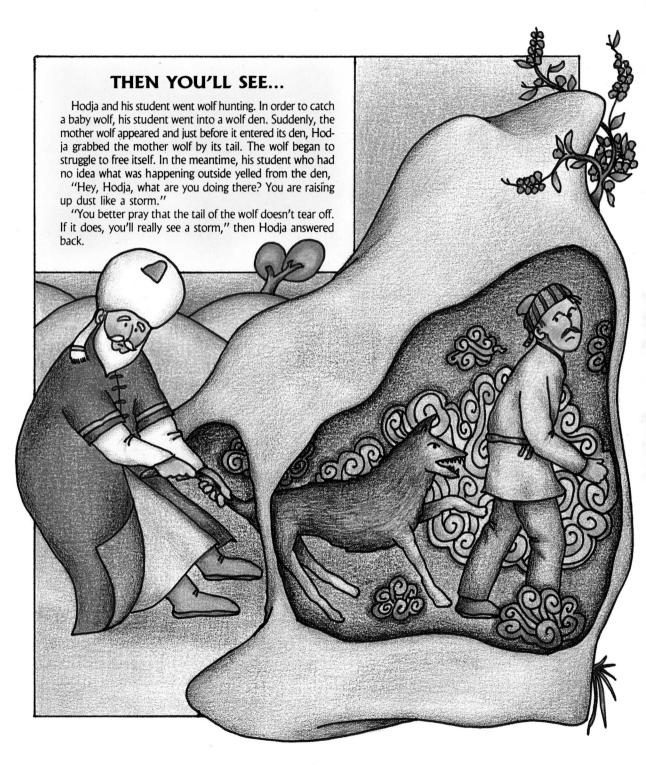

## THEN YOU'LL SEE...

Hodja and his student went wolf hunting. In order to catch a baby wolf, his student went into a wolf den. Suddenly, the mother wolf appeared and just before it entered its den, Hodja grabbed the mother wolf by its tail. The wolf began to struggle to free itself. In the meantime, his student who had no idea what was happening outside yelled from the den,

"Hey, Hodja, what are you doing there? You are raising up dust like a storm."

"You better pray that the tail of the wolf doesn't tear off. If it does, you'll really see a storm," then Hodja answered back.

## WHO IS GOING TO SELL THE PICKLES?

Hodja decided to become a pickle seller. He bought a donkey and other necessary items from an old pickle seller, and next day he started walking the streets to sell pickles. Since the donkey was experienced in selling pickles, everytime they passed by a house where they bought pickles, it brayed. Hodja was very eager to call out 'Pickles for sale' but the donkey wouldn't give him a chance. Each time Hodja opened his mouth to call out, the donkey brayed. Hodja punished the donkey a few times but in didn't help either. One day, he was in a crowded place and getting ready to shout 'Pickles for sale' but the donkey brayed again. Hodja was very disappointed. He turned to the donkey and said,

"Who is going to sell the pickles? You or me!"

## LOOK LIKE A BIRD

Hodja had never seen a stork before. When they gave him one and told him that it was a kind of bird, he gave it a strange look. He took it home, shortened its beak and legs, looked at it for awhile and then said to the stork,

"Good! Now, you look like a bird."

## FUNERAL IS COMING TO OUR HOUSE

Hodja was sitting by the window, and he saw a funeral procession coming down the street. Relatives of the deceased were crying and wailing,

"Oh! You are going to a dark place where there is no light or fire, no food or water. Oh!"

Hodja turned to his wife and said,

"Quick! Go and lock our door. They must be bringing the deceased to our house."

# I WILL NEVER MINGLE INTO YOUR AFFAIRS

One day, Hodja was riding to the next town. He was tired so he sat in the shade of a huge walnut tree. He took off his turban and his robe, too. He noticed pumpkins on the ground a few feet away. He looked at them for a while and said to himself, 'God sure works in strange ways. He makes these huge pumpkins grow on short grass and these small walnuts on tall trees with long branches'.

Suddenly, a walnut fell off the tree and hit Hodja on the head. He jumped up in pain, put his turban on and when his pain subsided, he looked up and said,

"Forgive me, God. I will never mingle into your affairs again. What would have happened to me if you had pumpkins growing on this tree..."

## WAS JUST GETTING USED TO

Financial situation of Hodja was getting worse everyday.. He began to cut down on everything, including the food he gave to his donkey. Since he noticed no change for the worse in the animal, he reduced the amount of food he gave him more everyday. One day the donkey died. Hodja was very sad.

"What a shame! Just as it was getting used to hunger, it died," he complained.

## WAS GOING TO GET DOWN ANYWAY

When one day Hodja fell off his donkey, children of the neighbourhood gathered around him and started making fun of him. They chanted,

"Hodja fell off the donkey, Hodja fell off the donkey."

Hodja pulled himself together and as though nothing had happened, he said nonchalantly,

"I was going to get down anyway."

## EVERY TIME I GOT ON

One day, Hodja loaded sacks of wheat on his donkey and was ready to take them to the mill when his neighbours saw him and asked him to take theirs, too. Hodja couldn't refuse. So he ended up with nine donkeys loaded with the sacks of wheat of nine households plus his own. It was difficult to keep the donkeys together. Before it got dark, he decided to count the donkeys. He counted nine. 'But where is mine? There should be ten', he said to himself. He got down from his donkey and counted again. There were ten. He got back on his donkey and continued on his way. To be sure, he decided to count again after awhile and there were nine. He got down from his donkey and recounted. Then there were ten. Finally, he said,

"I better walk. Every time I ride the donkey, there is one missing."

# EITHER YOU HAVE NEVER BEEN WHIPPED...

When Hodja was with Tamerlane, they brought in a drunk soldier and asked Tamerlane how to punish him.

"Give him three-hundred whips," Tamerlane ordered.

Hodja started laughing.

"Why are you laughing?" asked Tamerlane. "Are you making fun of me? You should be ashamed of yourself!"

"I am laughing because either you have never been whipped or you don't know how to count," Hodja replied.

# HEAR IT TOMORROW

One late night, Hodja and his friend were walking home. They saw thieves in front of the door of a store. One of the thieves was filing the lock to break it. Realizing he couldn't overcome the thieves, Hodja ignored them.

"What are these men doing so late in the night?" asked his friend.

"One of them is playing the rebab (a small string instrument) and the others are listening," Hodja answered.

His friend didn't take Hodja's remark seriously and said,

"But I cannot hear the rebab!"

Hodja smiled, and said,

"It will be heard tomorrow morning!"

# YOU TAKE THE MONEY

While Hodja was walking in the street somebody approached him and slapped him on the back of his neck. He was hurt badly so he wouldn't accept the man's apology. He took the man to the judge not knowing that the man was a close friend of him. The judge tried to convince Hodja to accept the man's apology but Hodja was adamant. The judge finally said,

"O.K. I have decided. This man will pay one akçe to Hodja," and signalled to the man,

"You go and bring the money."

The man left. Hodja waited and waited for the man to return and finally ran out of patience. He approached the judge who was reading the paper in front of him, and slapped him on the neck. He then told the judge,

"I have some business to attend to, so I am leaving. You go ahead and take the akçe in stead of me."

## DON'T HAVE IT

Hodja was busy repairing his roof when the doorbell rang. He looked down and saw a man at the door.

"What do you want," Hodja called out.

"Come down and I'll tell you," the man answered.

Hodja came down the stairs and opened the door. The man said,

"I need some money. Could you spare a few akçe?"

"Well, come up to the roof with me," Hodja replied.

When they climbed to the roof, Hodja turned to the man and said,

"I can't. I don't have any money."

The man was surprised.

"You could have told me that down there at the door," he said.

"Well," replied Hodja "You could have asked me while I was up here."

# FOLLOW THIS ROAD

Hodja climbed a tall tree, sat on a branch and started cutting the branch with an axe. A passerby saw him and yelled,

"What are you doing? You are going to fall down!"

Hodja ignored the man and kept on axing the branch he was sitting on. Finally, the branch broke and he fell on the ground. In spite of his scratches and bruises he got up and ran after the man.

"Hey, you! Since you knew I was going to fall down, you should be able to tell me when I will die," he told the man and wouldn't let him go without an answer. Finally, to get rid of Hodja, the man said,

"When your donkey brays twice in a row while carrying a heavy load of wood up a hill, you will die."

After awhile, when his donkey brayed twice in a row, Hodja said,

"That's it. I am dead," and threw himself on the ground.

The peasants who saw him there carried him to his house, washed him, put him in a casket and started taking him to the cemetery. The road they took divided into two and they didn't know which one led to the cemetery. They couldn't decide whether to take the one on the right or the left. Finally, Hodja lost his patience. He lifted up his head and said,

"Listen, when I was alive, I used to take this one to go to the cemetery."

# DID HE HAVE A HEAD?

Hodja went hunting wolves with his friend. They saw a big wolf and started chasing it but the wolf entered a cave. They waited for awhile and when it didn't come out, Hodja's friend stuck his head into the cave.

Hodja waited and then called out for him but didn't get an answer. Finally, he pulled his friend out by the legs, and found that his friend's head was missing! So, he left him there and returned to town. He went to his friend's house and asked his wife,

"Did your husband have a head when he left home this morning?"

# BY THE LIGHT OF AN OIL LAMP

One cold winter day, his friends decided to play a trick on Hodja to win a free meal. They told Hodja,

"If you can spend the whole night in the town square without a fire to warm you up, we will invite you to dinner but if you can't, then you will invite us. Is it a bet?"

Hodja agreed. He went to the square and found himself a place to spend the night. He was about to freeze but managed to spend the whole night there. His friends were surprised to find him in the square the next morning.

"How did you do it?" they asked.

"It was pitch dark so I sat here in the light of an oil lamp miles away," he replied.

"Oh, you cheated! You must have kept yourself warm in that light. So, you have to cook us a nice dinner," they told Hodja.

A few days later, they all went to Hodja's house. Hodja had a big cauldron hanging from a branch of a tall tree and below the cauldron he had lit a candle on the ground. His friends started getting anxious and asked,

"When is the dinner going to be ready?"

"As soon as the heat from the candle boils the water in the cauldron, I will start cooking your dinner," Hodja replied.

"That is impossible!" they exclaimed.

"But, why?" Hodja replied, "Just as the light of that weak oil lamp miles away kept me warm, the heat from his candle below the cauldron will boil the water."

## SOMETHING IS WRONG WITH THE HONEY

Hodja needed a court decree from the judge in Konya. He went to Konya to talk to the judge a few times but each tim
he was told to come back later. His frieds told Hodja that the judge was a very geedy man and that he would never get h
decree unless he bribed the judge.

Hodja listened to his friends advice and the next time he went to see the judge, he took along a big potful of honey. H
gave it to the judge and got the decree the same day.

That night, the judge wanted to taste the honey. When he dipped the spoon in the honey pot, he noticed that there wa
just a little honey only on top and the rest was mud. Next morning, he told the court officer,

"Find Hodja and bring him here. There are a few things wrong with the decree and they need to be corrected."

When the officer gave Hodja the judge's message, Hodja said calmly,

"Son, I know that there is nothing wrong with the decree, but there is something wrong with the pot of honey."

## DON'T BOTHER THE WOLF

One winter day, Hodja was cutting wood in the forest. A hungry wolf attacked his donkey he had left at the bottom of the hill, and devoured it. Somebody saw what happened and called out to Hodja,

"Come here, Hodja! A wolf ate your donkey and it is running up the hill."

Hodja looked at the remains of his poor donkey and said,

"Well, it is no use now. So, let's not bother the wolf that is trying to run up the hill on a full stomach."

## HOW FAR...

Hodja was running as fast and shouting as loud as he could. Somebody saw him and thought something had happened to him. So, he ran up to Hodja and asked,

"What happened, Hodja?"

Hodja kept on running and said,

"I wondered how far my voice travels. So, I am running after it."

## AFTER THE DAMAGE IS DONE

Hodja asked his son to go the fountain to get some water. He gave the boy the pitcher, slapped him on each cheek and said,

"Don't you break the pitcher!"

His neighbour who saw what happened, asked Hodja,

"What are you doing, Hodja? The boy hasn't broken the pitcher. So, why are you punishing the innocent child?"

"What good is punishing after the damage is done?" replied Hodja.

## IN THREE YEARS TIME

In order to teach Tamerlane's donkey to read, Hodja received three thousand gold pieces. According to the agreement, Hodja had three years to fulfill his promise.

"What did you do, Hodja? If you can't teach the donkey how to read Tamerlane will kill you," his friends warned him.

"Don't worry," Hodja replied. "In three years time, either the donkey or Tamerlane will be dead... Or may be even I will be dead, too."

## HAVEN'T WE MOVED

One night, a thief broke into Hodja's house. He gathered up everything, put them in a big sack and started carrying it away. Hodja, who was watching him from his bedroom, picked up the few items he had in the room and began to follow the thief. When they arrived to the thief's home, the thief noticed Hodja behind him.

He asked angrily,

"What are you doing here, in my house?"

"Why are you so surprised?" Hodja replied. "Aren't we moving into this house?"

## IF THE WRONG IS NOT KNOWN

When they asked Hodja to show where his nose is, he pointed at the back of his neck.

"But you are pointing at the wrong side," they said.

"If you don't know the wrong, you can never tell the right," Hodja replied.

## USE AS WEIGHTS

While plowing, Hodja discovered a pot full of gold coins. He couldn't decide whether to keep the pot or give it to the judge. 'Well, I am not going to leave it here. That's for sure', he said to himself and put it in his bag to take it home.

When his wife felt that the bag was heavier than usual, she opened it to see what was in it. She took the gold pieces, replaced them with stones and tied the bag again.

That night, Hodja thought and thought and finally decided to give the pot of gold to the judge. Next morning, he took the bag and went to see the judge.

He took the pot off the bag, turned it upside down and when he saw the stones spread on the table in stead of the gold pieces, he was shocked but remained calm.

"Hodja, what are these?" asked the surprised judge.

Hodja acted as though there was nothing unusual and said,

"I thought you might like to make weights with them to give to the venders in the marketplace to use."

## KNOW HOW TO SWIM

Hodja's wife was getting old and ugly so he decided to get married again and have a second wife. He married a young and beautiful lady. Of course, the wives were so jealous of each other that they fought often. One day, they decided to find out which one Hodja loved the best and asked him,

"Let's say that one day we were sailing in the lake. Suddenly a storm broke out and our boat capsized. Which one of us would you save first?"

Hodja tried to ignore the question but they insisted for an answer. Hodja then turned to his first wife and said,

"You know how to swim a little, don't you?"

## ONE WHO GIVES THE MONEY

When Hodja was on his way to the marketplace, children of the nighbourhood gathered around him and asked him to buy each one a whistle. Hodja agreed and as he was leaving, one of the children gave him the money for his whistle.

In the evening, when Hodja returned from the marketplace, the children surrounded him and asked him whether he had bought whistles for them. He took out one whistle from his pocket, gave it to the child who had given him the money and said, "The one who pays gets   to blow the whistle!"

## NEED A ROOSTER

Hodja went to a Turkish bath with some of the children in the neighbourhood. While they were sitting on the marble slab in the bath, the children said,

"Let's each one lay an egg! The one who can't, will pay the bill."

Each one cackled like a chicken and placed the egg he had brought with him on the marble slab. When Hodja saw what was happening, he kept calm and after a few minutes he started acting and crowing like a rooster. The children were surprised.

"What are you doing, Hodja?" they asked.

"Well, don't you think that there should be a rooster for all these chickens," he answered.

## IF I WERE IN IT

One night, Hodja heard noises coming from his garden and when he looked out the window, he saw someone dressed in white. He woke up his wife and asked her to bring his bow and arrow.

"There is a thief in the garden and I am going to shoot him," he said.

In moonlight, he took an aim at the man, shot him and said,

"Let's go back to sleep. We will take care of him in the morning."

Next morning, he went into the garden looking for the dead thief but he found out that what he had shot wasn't a man but his white shirt which his wife had hung out to dry.

"Thank God!" he exclaimed.

"Why are you thanking God?" his wife asked.

"Don't you see, the arrow went right through the chest. What would have happened if I were wearing the shirt," he replied.

## WHERE IT BELONGS

On a moonlit night Hodja went to the well to get some water.

When he looked down he saw the reflection of the full moon. 'I must save the moon', he said to himself and dropped the hook used for rescuing buckets into the well. The hook got caught onto something. He began to pull on the rope as hard as he could. The rope snapped and Hodja fell on his back. He was hurt but when he opened his eyes and saw the moon in the sky, he exclaimed,

"Thank God! I tried hard but finally the moon is back where it belongs."

## MY LEGS SHOOK

Hodja's wife was very difficult to live with. She used to nag all the time and Hodja got fed up. During one of his sermons he talked about nagging wives and poured his heart out. When he was finished, he felt much better and asked the men in the congregation, who had nagging wives, to stand up. Every man stood up and he was very surprised. One of his frieds remarked,

"Hodja, only you didn't stand up. You must be very happy with your wife!"

"Oh, no!" replied Hodja, "I was going to stand up before everybody else but when the subject came up I got so excited that my legs started shaking and I couldn't even move."

## HAVEN'T WE MOVED

One night, a thief broke into Hodja's house. He gathered up everything, put them in a big sack and started carrying it away. Hodja, who was watching him from his bedroom, picked up the few items he had in the room and began to follow the thief. When they arrived to the thief's home, the thief noticed Hodja behind him. He asked angrily,

"What are you doing here, in my house?"

"Why are you surprised?" Hodja replied.

"Aren't we moving into this house?"

## SHALL I MOVE MORE

One night in bed Hodja's wife asked him,

"Would you move away to give me more space?"

Hodja got up, put his shoes on and started walking down the street. After he walked about two hours he met a friend. Following the usual greetings, Hodja said,

"When you arrive in Akşehir, go to my house and ask my wife wheather she wants me to move more?"

## DEAD ONWER

When Hodja asked,
"How can you tell that a man is dead?"
"His hands and feet get as cold as ice," they answered.

One cold winter day, while he was cutting wood in the forest he realized that his hands and feet were as cold as ice. He thought he was dead and stretched out on the snow.

Soon, hungry wolves attacked his donkey, tore it apart and began devouring it. Hodja couldn't bear sight the anymore.. He lifted up his head and called out to the wolves,

"Go ahead, help yourselves now that you have found a helpless donkey with a dead owner."

# NO CHANGE

One day, Hodja was riding his donkey. A passerby asked him, 'Hodja, how many legs does your donkey have?"
Hodja came down his donkey, counted its legs one by one and said, "It has four legs."
People who heard the conversation asked,
"Hodja, don't you know how many legs your donkey has?"
"Of course I know," Hodja answered. "But, the last time I counted them was last night and I just wanted to make sure that nothing had changed."

# THIRD YEAR

During Ramadan, they asked Hodja,
"Does kissing your wife break the fast?"
Hodja smiled and said,
"If you are newly married, then it does break the fast.. If you are married for two years... Well, that I don't know but if you are married for three years, then you don't kiss your wife anyway. But even if you do, you won't be breaking your fast!"

# NOT EVEN GETTING DOWN

Hodja went to the pulpit to deliver his sermon but couldn't find a subject to talk about.
"Well, I came up here to give a sermon but I can't think of thing to talk about," he said.
His son called out from the floor,
"Can't you even think of coming down the pulpit, father?"

## YOU BELIEVE THE DONKEY...

One of Hodja's friends wanted to borrow his donkey for a day·to go to the mill but Hodja told him that it wasn't there that day. Just as he finished his sentence the donkey started braying in the shed.

"Apparently your donkey is in the shed. I am disappointed in you. You won't let an old friend like me to borrow even your donkey," his neighbour complained.

Hodja raised his voice and said,

"You are a strange man! You don't believe an old, respectable man like me but you go ahead and believe a donkey!"

## THIS ONE THINKS

While strolling in the marketplace, Hodja saw a colourful bird for sale for twelve gold pieces. He was very curious and asked,

"Why is this bird so expensive?"

"This is a parrot and it talks," replied the seller.

Hodja went straight home, grabbed his turkey and went back to the marketplace to sell it.

"How much do you want for the turkey?" they asked.

"Ten gold pieces," answered Hodja.

Everybody was shocked.

"Turkeys don't cost that much!" they remarked.

"Well, that man is asking twelve gold pieces for that bird," Hodja said.

"But Hodja, that parrot has a skill. It talks. What does your turkey do?"

"If that parrot talks then this turkey thinks!" replied Hodja.

## FROM THE OTHER WORLD

One day, when he was in the cemetery, Hodja took off his clothes to shake the dust off of them. A gust of wind blew his shirt and while he was running after it, he came across a few riders. The horses were scared by Hodja's sudden appearance and became difficult to control. The riders were quite upset. They yelled at Hodja,

"What are you doing like this in a cemetery? Are you a ghost or something?"

Hodja answered calmly,

"My sons, I come from the other world. I need to relieve myself. So, in order not to get the other world dirty either, I came out of my grave. As soon as I relieve myself, I'll go back."

## SOUND ASLEEP

Hodja had a short and narrow quilt. On cold nights, he used to pile his robe and sweaters on his quilt and try to keep warm. One snowy night, Hodja's wife was very cold and couln't sleep. She tossed and turned in the bed and by her nagging kept Hodja awake. Finally, he got off the bed, went to the garden, filled a sack with snow and brought it to his wife.

"Here," he said. "I brought you a sackful of snow. Make a quilt or whatever you want to keep you warm."

"Are you crazy?" his wife replied. "They don't make quilts from snow. Snow doesn't keep you warm!"

"It sure does!" Hodja said. "If it didn't, would your grandparents be sleeping soundly under it for thousands of years?"

## I HAVE THE RECIPE

Hodja bought a big piece of liver and on his way home he met a friend who gave him a new recipe for a delicious liver dish. Hodja was so impressed by the recipe that he asked his friend to write it down on a piece of paper so he wouldn't forget it. As he was walking home thinking about the recipe and the delicious dish he was going to have that night, a crow grabbed the piece if liver off his hands and flew away. Hodja looked after the bird for a while and then said,

"Your dinner is not going to be as delicious as the one I was going to have because I have the recipe."

## YOU WERE DIFFERENT

Hodja gave his donkey to a broker to sell it. Next day, the broker told Hodja,

"I couldn't sell your donkey. They took it to Konya and made it the judge."

Hodja was mad so he decided to go to Konya and tell the judge what had happened.

The judge had the broker found and brought to him. He reprimanded the broker and told him,

"Find Hodja's donkey and bring it here within one hour or else only God knows what I'll do with you!"

The broker was scared. He went to the market, bought a donkey and brought it to Hodja.

Hodja looked at the donkey, then at the judge, then back at the donkey. The judge was curious.

"Why do you keep on looking at the donkey, and me, Hodja? Don't you like it?" he asked.

"I do, I do," Hodja answered, "but you sure were different, though!"

## ONLY THOSE WHO SLEEP ON ROOF TOPS

One hot summer night, Hodja was resting in bed with his wife on the roof. They began to fight. Hodja was mad. He got up and said,

"I am fed up. You don't let me rest peacefully even in bed." As he walked away, he lost his balance and fell off the edge of the roof.

The neighbours, who heard the noises, came to his rescue.

"What happened how do you feel, Hodja?" they asked.

Hodja tried to pull himself together and said,

"Only those who sleep on roof tops, fight with their wives and fall off the edge of a roof can understand how I feel now."

## MONEY FOR TROUSERS

While he was in Bursa, Hodja went to the marketplace to buy a pair of trousers. He chose one pair but just before he paid for them he told the seller that he changed his mind and wanted to buy a robe in stead. He picked a robe and started walking away but the seller stop ped him.

"Hodja, you haven't paid for the robe," he said.

"Well, I returned the pair of trousers and bought the robe in stead," Hodja replied.

"But you hadn't paid for the trousers, either," remarked the seller.

Hodja got mad.

"You are a strange man! You expect me to pay for a pair of trousers I didn't buy!"

# MULES CARRYING POTS AND PANS

As he was passing by a cemetery one day, Hodja noticed an empty grave. He said to himself, 'I wonder wheather angels would come and interrogate me if I lie down there looking dead, and stretched out in the grave. Soon, he heard clanking and banging.

"My God! The world is coming to an end," he said and jumped off the grave. He saw mules carrying pots and pans. Apparently, they were making all that noise.

When the mules, alarmed the sudden appearance of Hodja, started running aimlessly, all the pots and pans they were carrying fell off of them and were broken. The owners of the mules were furious.

"Who are you? What are you doing here?" they yelled.

"I came here from the other world to see what is happening," Hodja replied.

"We'll show you what is happening," they said and started hitting and kicking Hodja until he passed out.

When Hodja came to himself, he began to walk home. He had scratches and bruises all over his body and his clothes were all torn apart. When people saw him, they asked what had happened.

"Oh, don't ask! I was dead... I am coming from the other world," he said.

"Oh, yes! Well, how are things over there?" they inquired. Hodja was in pain and he could only say,

"If you don't scare mules carrying pots and pans, everything is allright."

## INNOCENT THIEF

Hodja's donkey was stolen. In stead of consoling, his neighbours were blaming him saying,

"You should have locked the shed,"

"Didn't you hear any noises?"

"You should have tied the donkey securely."

Hodja listened patiently, for awhile and finally said,

"Well, you are putting all the blame on me.. Do you think the thief was innocent?"

# 49th OF RAMADAN

In order to keep track of the days of the month of Ramadan, Hodja used to drop a pebble into a bucket each day, and whenever he wanted to know which day of Ramadan it was, he used to count the pebbles. When his mischevious neighbour found out about Hodja's method, he added pebbles into Hodja's bucket and next day asked Hodja which day of Ramadan it was.

Hodja went to his bucket and counted the pebbles in it. There were 149 of them. 'This is too much!' he said to himself. Then he came back and said,

"Today is the 49th of Ramadan."

His mischevious neighbour remarked,

"But, Hodja, how can it be? There aren't 49 days in Ramadan."

Hodja replied with a smile on his face,

"49 is nothing. According to the pebbles method, today is the 149th of Ramadan."

# WHOEVER HAS THE BLUE BEAD

Hodja had two wives and they used to fight quite often due to jealousy. To put an end to these fightings, Hodja gave each one a blue bead and said,

"Now, don't tell the other one that I gave you this bead which is a symbol of my love for you."

One day they were fighting again. They asked Hodja whom he loved the best. He answered calmly,

"I love the who has the blue bead."

Each wife thought Hodja loved her the best and never bothered him again.

## IF IT WEARS THESE

Hodja wanted a job as a preacher, during the Ramadan so he visited every town in the vicinity. Since each town had a preacher, he couldn't find a job and decided to go back to his home town. On the way, he stopped at a village and noticed that there were people yelling and screaming in the village square. He was curious, so he asked what was happening. They pointed at a wolf tied up securely and said,

"This horrible animal killed every chicken and rooster in town. We finally caught it but can't decide how to punish it."

"Leave it to me," Hodja said. As the peasants watched curiously, Hodja took off his robe and turban and put them on the wolf.

"We don't understand it, Hodja. What kind of a punishment is this?" they asked.

"Don't worry," Hodja said. "When the people in other towns see it in these clothes, they won't let it come near their town, so it will die of hunger."

## WHY HE COUGHED

Hodja and his wife were awakened one night by the sound of footsteps and they heard someone say,

"Let's kill Hodja and his sheep, take his belongings and kidnap his wife."

Upon hearing this, Hodja coughed a few times and the noise stopped. A few minutes later, his wife said,

"I assume you got scared and coughed,"

Hodja was furious.

"You were fine! I coughed for myself and my sheep," he said.

## IT DOESN'T MAKE ANY DIFFERENCE

They asked Hodja whether one should walk ahead of a casket or follow it during a funeral procession.

Hodja answered,

"As long as you are not in it, it doesn't make any difference."

## WHEN YOU WERE YOUNG...

Hodja wanted to ride a horse. The animal was tall. Although he attempted a few times, Hodja couldn't mount the horse. When he fell on the ground on his final try, he was embarrassed. To make sure that the people around him heard him clearly, he said loudly,

"Oh, old age! Was I like this in my youth," and then he murmured to himself,

"Come on, I knew you when you were young, too"

## DO AS YOU PLEASE

Hodja and his son were going to another village. His son was riding the donkey and Hodja was walking along. A few people were coming down the road. They stopped and pointing at his son they muttered,

"Look at that! The poor old man is walking and the young boy is riding the donkey. The youth of today has no consideration!" Hodja was irritated. He told his son to come down, and he began to ride the donkey himself. Then, they saw another group of people, who remarked:

"Look at that man! On a hot day like this, he is riding the donkey and the poor boy is walking."

So, Hodja pulled his son on the donkey, too. After awhile, they saw a few more people coming down the road.

"Poor animal! Both of them are riding on it and it is about to pass out."

Hodja was fed up. He and his son got down and started walking behind the donkey. Soon, they heard a few people say,

"Look at those stupid people. They have a donkey but won't ride it."

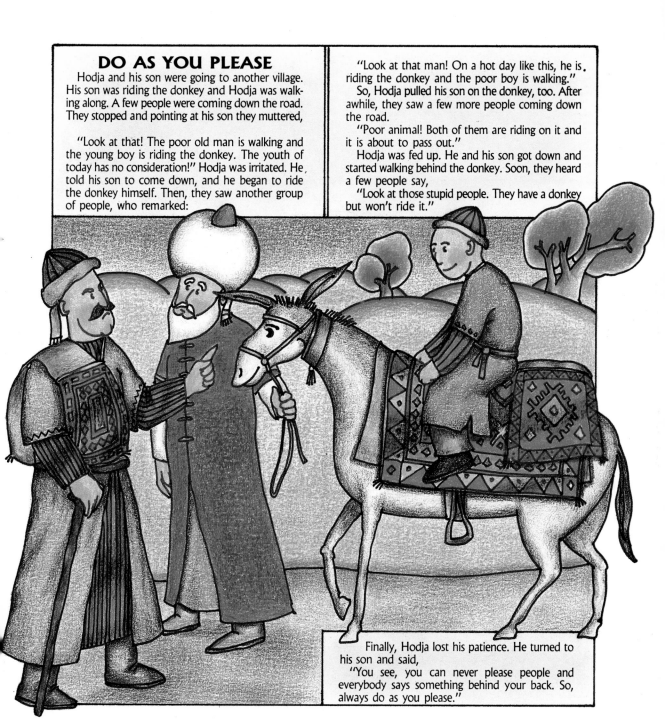

Finally, Hodja lost his patience. He turned to his son and said,

"You see, you can never please people and everybody says something behind your back. So, always do as you please."

## IT IS BETTER...

One day, Hodja's wife baked his favorite dessert. They ate most of it and saved the rest for breakfast.

That night, Hodja couldn't fall a sleep. He woke up his wife and said, "Wake up, wake up! I have something important to tell you."

While his sleepy wife was trying to get up, Hodja rushed to the kitchen, brought the left over dessert and told his wife,

"Let's finish this. It's better to have it in our stomach than in our mind."

## WHEREVER IT TAKES ME!

Hodja had to go to one of the villages nearby. He got on his mule but the animal was very disobedient that day. In stead of going in the direction Hodja led it, the mule went where it wanted. Also, it ran for awhile, then stopped, then ran again.. Hodja was fed up. So, when a friend he met on the road asked,

"Have a good trip, Hodja. Where are you going?," Hodja answered, "Wherever this mule takes me!"

## BE A KITE FOR A YEAR

When they asked Hodja,

"Is it true that a kite (a kind of bird) spends six months of the year as female and the other six months as male?"

"In order to answer that question one has to be a kite for a year," he answered.

## I FELT SORRY

When they saw Hodja riding on his donkey and carrying a big sack on his back, they were curious and asked,

"Hey, Hodja, why are you carrying the sack on your own back?"

"Well, the poor animal is tired and now he is carrying me. So, I felt sorry for him and decided to save him the extra burden," he aswered.

## YOU BELIEVED THAT IT GAVE BIRTH...

Hodja had borrowed his neighbour's cauldron. A few days later, he put a bowl in it and returned it. When his neighbour saw the bowl, he asked,

"What is this?"

Hodja answered,

"Your cauldron gave birth!"

His neighbour was very happy. He thanked Hodja and took the cauldron and the bowl.

A few weeks later, Hodja borrowed the cauldron again but this time he didn't return it. When his neighbour came to ask for it, Hodja said,

"Your cauldron died. I am sorry."

The man was surprised.

"Oh, come on!" he said, "Cauldrons don't die."

Hodja snapped back,

"Well, you believed that it gave birth, then why don't you believe that it died?"

## BEHIND THE MOUNTAIN

Hodja was whistling a happy tune while looking for his lost donkey. Intrigued by Hodja's strange behavior, his friend asked,

"Hodja, a person who looses something important gets upset. But here you are singing a happy tune. Why?"

"My last hope lies behind this mountain, and if don't find my donkey there either, then watch how I wail!" Hodja replied.

## CAN SMELL FANTACIES

Hodja had a yen for a delicious bowl of soup with lots of yogurt and mint leaves in it. 'I wish I had a bowl of soup I could sip', he was thinking when the doorbell rang. It was the neighbour's son with a bowl in his hand.

"My father says, 'Hello' and wants to borrow a bowl of soup, if you have some," he said.

Hodja smiled and said,

"Well! My neighbours can smell even my fantacies."

## TURN INSIDE OUT

On the way to Konya, Hodja met a friend who had never been there before. They started walking together and as they got close to the town his friend noticed the tall minarets and was very impressed by them.

"How do they build them so tall?" he asked.

Hodja was in a mischevious mood. He smiled and said,

"They turn deep wells inside out."

## NONE OF YOUR BUSINESS

While Hodja was strolling in the marketplace one day, a busybody approached him and said,

"Hey, Hodja, I saw someone carrying a big plateful of delicious baklava."

"None of my business," said Hodja nonchalantly.

"But Hodja, he was carrying it to your house," the man continued.

"Then it is none of your business," Hodja snapped back.

## FLOUR ON THE ROPE

His neighbour wanted to borrow Hodja's rope. Hodja went into his house and when he came out after awhile, he told his neighbour,
"We are using the rope. My wife has laid flour on it."
His neighbour was surprised.
"That's impossible! You can't lay flour on a rope!"
"If you don't want to lend it, then it is possible," Hodja remarked..

## I DID NOT LIKE IT EITHER

When they asked Hodja whether he ever invented something,
"Yes, I did," he answered. "I invented eating bread and snow, but even I didn't like it."

## MYSTERIOUS WAYS

Hodja had his money stolen. He was quite upset and prayed often to find it. In the mean time, the ship one of the wealthy residents of Akşehir was sailing was caught in a storm. The man was so scared that he promised himself to give two-hundred akçes to Hodja if he got safely back home.

He survived the storm, and when he returned home he gave two-hundred akçes to Hodja as he had promised. Of course, Hodja was thrilled. He thought for a few minutes and then said,
"My Lord, such coincidences! You sure work in mysterious ways."

(Akçe: Silver coin used during the Ottoman Empire).

(Akçe: Silver coin used during the Ottoman Empire)

# BIBLIOGRAPHIE

**Ali Nuri:** *Nasreddin Khodjas schwanke und streiche Turkische Gescliten aus Timurlenks Tagen*, Illustr. Anthur Gjögren - Wald Undersen, Breslau 1904.

**Bater, William Burchardt:** *Pleasing Tales of Khoja Nasr-iddeen Efendi*, A Reading Book of Turkish Language, London 1854.

**Barnham, Henry Rudley:** *The Khoja: Tales of Nasr-ed-din*, New York, 1924, (Illustrated).

**Burrill, Kathleen R.F.:** *The Nasreddin Hodja Stories*, New York 1957.

**Decourdemanche, J.A.:** *Sottisier de Nasr-Eddin Hodja. Bouffon de Tamerlan, suivi d'autres facéites turques, traduits sur des manuscrits inédits*, Brüksel 1878.

*Büyük Nasreddin Hoca*, Maarif Kütüphanesi, İst. 1954, (Illustrated).

**Decourdemanche, J.A.:** *Sottisier de Nasr-Eddin Hodja. Bouffon de Tamerlan, suivi d'autres facéites turques, traduits sur des manuscrits inédits*, Brüksel 1878.

**Gordlevskiy, V.A.:** *Anekdoti o Hoca Nasr-Ed-Dine*. Moskova-Leningrad 1936.

**Gordlevskogo, V.A.:** *Anekdoti o Hodja Nasreddine*, Moskova 1957.

**Gökşen, Enver Hacı:** *Hoca'dan Fıkralar*, İyigün Yayınevi, İst. 1964.

**Gölpınarlı, Abdülbaki:** *Nasreddin Hoca*, Resimleyen: Abidin Dino, Remzi Kitabevi, İst. 1961, 112 s.

**Güney, Eflatun Cem:** *Nasreddin Hoca Fıkraları*, Yeditepe Yayınları, İst. 1957, (Illustrated).

**Kabacalı, Alpay:** *Bütün Yönleriyle Nasreddin Hoca*, Özgür Yayın Dağıtım, İst. 1991.

**Kanık, Orhan Veli:** *Nasreddin Hoca (70 Manzum Hikâye)*, Doğan Kardeş Yayınları, İst. 1949.

**Karahasan, Mustafa:** *Nasreddin Hodza i Njegov Humor*, Belgrad 1959.

**Köprülü, Fuat:** *Manzum Nasreddin Hoca Fıkraları*, Haz.: Dr. Atâ Çatıkbaş, Üçdal Yayınları, İst. 1980.

**Kunos, Dr. Ignacz:** *Anecdotes of Nasr-Eddin*, Budapeşte 1899.

**Mahen, Jiri:** *Janosik ulicka odvahy Nasreddin*, Prag 1962, 310 s.

**Mallouf, N.::** *Plaisanteries de Nasr-Eddin Khodja*, İzmir 1854.

*Molla Nasreddin Lâtifeleri*, Bakû 1966.

**Nesin, Aziz:** *The Tales of Nasrettin Hoca*, Retold in English by Talât Halman, Dost Yayınları, İst. 1988, (Illustrated).

*Nevâdir-i Nasreddini'r-Rûmiyy-il meşhur be Cuhâ*, Kahire 1278/1862.

**Önder, Mehmet:** *Nasreddin Hoca*, İş Bankası Kültür Yayınları, İst. 1971.

**Pann, Anton:** *Nastratin Hogea*, Bükreş 1908.

**Pio, V.:** *Lustiger historier om Nasreddin Hodja*, Kopenhag 1902.

**Ramazani, Muhammed:** *Molla Nasroddin*, Tahran 1319/1940.

**Solovev, Leonid:** *Povest o Hodja Nasreddine*, Moskova 1957, 1+191 s.

**Spies, Dr. Otto:** *Hodscha Nasreddin. Ein Turkisher Eulenspiegel*, Berlin 1928.

**Şop, İvan:** *Nasreddinove Metamorfoze*, Belgrad 1973, 148 s.

**Tahmasip, M.T.:** *Molla Nasreddin Lâtifeleri*, Bakû 1965.

**Tokmakçıoğlu, Erdoğan:** *Bütün Yönleriyle Nasreddin Hoca*, Sinan Yayınları, İst. 1971.

**Wesselski, Albert:** *Der Hodscha Nasreddin, Türkische, arabische, berberische, maltesische, sizilianische, kalabrische, kroatische, serbische und griechische Marlein und Schwanke*, Weimar 1911.

**Yeşim, Ragıp Şevki:** *Dünyayı Güldüren Adam Nasreddin Hoca*, Bütün fıkraları ve hayatının romanı, 6 cilt birarada, Hadise Yayınevi, İst. 1956, (Illustrated).

**Zimmanichi, N.:** *Vyber tekstov Tureckion opo vidania Choday Nasreddina*, Varşova 1951.

# PUBLICATION LIST

**TURKEY (BN)** *(In English, French, German, Italian, Spanish, Dutch)*
**ANCIENT CIVILIZATIONS AND RUINS OF TURKEY**
*(In English)*
**ISTANBUL (B)** *(In English, French, German, Italian, Spanish, Japanese)*
**ISTANBUL (ORT)** *(In English, French, German, Italian, Spanish)*
**ISTANBUL (BN)** *(In English, French, German, Italian, Spanish, Japanese)*
**MAJESTIC ISTANBUL** *(In English, German)*
**TURKISH CARPETS** *(In English, French, German, Italian, Spanish, Japanese)*
**TURKISH CARPETS** *(In English, German)*
**THE TOPKAPI PALACE** *(In English, French, German, Italian, Italian, Spanish, Japanese, Turkish)*
**HAGIA SOPHIA** *(In English, French, German, Italian, Spanish)*
**THE KARİYE MUSEUM** *(In English, French, German, Italian, Spanish)*
**ANKARA** *(In English, French, German, Italian, Spanish, Turkish)*
**Unique CAPPADOCIA** *(In English, French, German, Italian, Spanish, Japanese, Turkish)*
**CAPPADOCIA (BN)** *(In English, French, German, Italian, Spanish, Dutch, Turkish)*
**EPHESUS** *(In English, French, German, Italian, Spanish, Japanese)*
**EPHESUS (BN)** *(In English, French, German, Italian, Spanish, Dutch)*
**APHRODISIAS** *(In English, French, German, Italian, Spanish, Turkish)*
**THE TURQUOISE COAST OF TURKEY** *(In English)*
**PAMUKKALE (HIERAPOLIS)** *(In English, French, German, Italian, Spanish, Dutch, Japanese, Turkish)*
**PAMUKKALE (BN)** *(In English, French, German, Italian, Spanish)*
**PERGAMON** *(In English, French, German, Italian, Spanish, Japanese)*
**LYCIA (AT)** *(In English, French, German)*
**KARIA (AT)** *(In English, French, German)*
**ANTALYA (BN)** *(In English, French, German, Italian, Dutch, Turkish)*
**PERGE** *(In English, French, German)*
**ASPENDOS** *(In English, French, German)*
**ALANYA** *(In English, French, German, Turkish)*
**The Capital of Urartu: VAN** *(In English, French, German)*
**TRABZON** *(In English, French, German, Turkish)*
**TURKISH COOKERY** *(In English, French, German, Italian, Spanish, Dutch, Japanese, Turkish)*
**NASREDDİN HODJA** *(In English, French, German, Italian, Spanish, Japanese)*
**TÜRKÇE-JAPONCA KONUŞMA KILAVUZU** *(Japanese-Turkish)*
**ANADOLU UYGARLIKLARI** *(Turkish)*

## *MAPS*

**TURKEY (NET), TURKEY (ESR), TURKEY (WEST)**
**TURKEY (SOUTH WEST), ISTANBUL, MARMARİS,**
**ANTALYA-ALANYA, ANKARA, İZMİR, CAPPADOCIA**

# NET® BOOKSTORES

ISTANBUL
Galleria Ataköy, Sahil Yolu, 34710 Ataköy - Tel: (9-1) 559 09 50
Ramada Hotel, Ordu Caddesi, 226, 34470 Laleli - Tel: (9-1) 513 64 31
İZMİR
Cumhuriyet Bulvarı, 142/B, 35210 Alsancak - Tel: (9-51) 21 26 32

ISBN 975-479-123-6